For the real Rob and Matt.
Remember, these characters are,
for better or worse,
fictional.

Chapter One

The problem with my brother is that he is far too often full of it. Which is why I was skeptical when he said he'd landed me a DJ gig at the local all-ages club.

"Friday night," he said.

"Seriously, Adam, don't mess with me right now." I was in my room trying to beat-match an old soul record with a white label drum-and-bass LP. It was not going well.

"I'm serious, Rob. I got you this Friday night!"

"Adam," I said, taking my headphones off and silencing the stereo. "DJ Sly does Friday nights at The Disco." DJ Sly was a ridiculous name for a DJ. The Disco was a ridiculous name for an all-ages club. And yet, at that time, I would have done anything to be DJ Sly playing at The Disco. Proving yet again that life, at its core, is a cruel joke.

"Do you mean the DJ Sly who just recently took a nasty tumble and busted his wrist? That DJ Sly?"

"What?" I said. "I never heard about that."

"That's because it happened yesterday, and you, as far as I can tell, have been locked in here for the past week." He looked at the floor, where there were piles of dirty plates and glasses. Mom had been working double shifts, leaving the two of us to our own devices.

Always a bad idea.

Adam is taller than me by about three inches. He's also thicker. I've never been able to break 120, pounds while Adam is a steady 160. He is far too fond of hair gel. His black curls are totally glued to his head. I have longer hair and let it do what it wants. And yet there's always talk about how we look so much alike. Adam has small eyes, which some people might refer to as beady. And his nose is a little too big for the rest of his face. It's these kinds of characteristics that people seem to become depressed about. Like, there's nothing you can do about the size of your eyes or nose, but people are going to make you feel bad about it anyway. Adam also had some pretty severe acne for a while, and his constant action against the angry red balls has left his skin pockmarked and rutted.

In the end, though, neither of us are hideous. But Adam has cared too much for too long about how he looks, and now he often walks hunched over with a hoodie pulled up around his face. Though I have noticed that in the past few months, he's begun to stand a little straighter.

"Anyway, Sly is down for the count and he needs a replacement."

"And how did you get me Sly's night?" I dropped my headphones around my neck. I then cleared a bunch of records off my bed to make room to sit down.

"I've been working there. You know that." Adam leaned against the door frame and examined a fingernail.

"So you've been saying. What, exactly, is your job?"

"This and that. What does it matter? I got you the night, Rob. You can do this, right? I haven't just made myself look like an ass on your account, have I?"

I looked at my crates of LPs. A lot of DJs had moved onto digital MP3 turntables. But MP3s sound awful, in my opinion. When you put a poorly encoded song through a giant system like they have at The Disco, it sounds like you're listening to music underwater. Everything is floppy and round-sounding. Records are crisp. The beats, hard.

Besides, I can't afford a laptop to run it all.

"For sure," I said, sounding as confident as possible.

"It's a big night, man," Adam said. He hadn't moved from the doorway. I knew exactly why. He wanted to be thanked for his awesomeness.

"Yeah, it'll be huge. Thanks, man."

"No problem." He swiveled off the door frame and put his fist out in front of him. I gave it a quick pump.

"How long is my set?"

"Three hours. You go on at nine. DJ Lookie takes over at midnight."

"Awesome," I said, getting excited about it. "Thanks, man. Seriously."

The next thing I did was call Matt.

"He's probably dicking you around, Rob," Matt said.

"Really? What's he going to do, suddenly tell me it was a joke when I show up with my gear?" I opened my curtains and was surprised to find it sunny out. I guess I did spend too much time in this small, dark room.

"Like that would be a surprise?" Adam had tied Matt to a tree with a skipping rope once, when we were all kids. Matt had been unable to ever forgive him. On a fairly regular basis, I heard about what an ass my brother was. Though after I punched Matt in the gut once, he tended to keep it to himself unless we were on the phone.

"Why do you have to be such a douche?"

"I'll believe it when you're in the DJ booth. Not a second before," Matt said.

"It's going to happen, Matt. And by the way, you're driving me."

"I don't go to The Disco. That place is way too lame."

"And what great plans do you have for Friday night?" I asked.

"Nothing yet, but something will come around."

"Nothing ever comes around, Matt. You're driving me. I'll get you backstage."

"Backstage at The Disco? Oh, my prayers have been answered! Christmas has come early! My next five birthdays have been squished into a little ball and rolled down the hallway of happiness. Backstage at The Disco!"

"Shut up. Maybe I'll let you up in the booth. You can flick a light on and off all night."

"Can it be a green light?" Matt said.

"Think you can handle two lights? I might let you at a red one as well."

"It *is* Christmas!" Matt said. "Hey, I just had a thought."

"Jesus, man, hold on to it. In *your* head, a thought is as rare as a diamond." Matt ignored my comment. He's useless at comebacks.

"You know who has recently been spotted at The Disco?"

"Who?" I said. I hadn't been to the club in over a month.

"Mary Jane McNally."

"How do you know that?" I said way too quickly.

"I hear things. Apparently, she dresses far less reserved than at school."

"Mary Jane McNally is God's gift to Resurrection Falls, Matt. Whatever she decides to clothe herself in has been preordained from on high. And those lips. Those beautiful, thick lips. They look as though they've been inflated."

"You have it bad, man."

"You are my ride. This is going to happen." I hung up before he could say another word.

Chapter Two

"That's my name," I said. "Can you see it?" Matt's dilapidated Jetta was one of only four cars in The Disco's parking lot.

"It's covered in crud," Matt said. Which it was. Whoever had put the letters in the billboard had dropped one and neglected to clean it off. "It looks like it says Rob olo."

"It says Rob Solo," I said. Before I had clued into the fact that once you have a DJ name you have to keep it, I'd called myself Rob Solo after Han Solo in *Star Wars*. I guess it was a cool enough name. But even if it wasn't, I was stuck with it.

"You have selected a beautiful evening to make your debut," Matt said. The snow had been coming down for hours. Though it did make this otherwise dull gray city look halfway nice.

"I have," I said, opening the car door. "Now help me get this junk inside."

"What's all this shit?" Ernie, the owner of The Disco, asked.

"My records," I said. "And turntables." Matt was trying to keep his portion of the load upright, but his arms were like twigs.

"I gotta put this down," he said.

"I have turntables," Ernie said. He seemed really annoyed with me. "Have you never played a club before? Everyone else shows up with a computer or a little hard drive."

"I don't use MP3s," I said. I noticed Adam coming across the dance floor toward us.

"Why not?" he asked.

I looked at my feet. "Sound quality," I said.

"What are you talking about? You think my system is shit?" Ernie said.

"No, I mean…"

"I'm seriously going to drop this stuff," Matt said.

"Hey, Rob," Adam said. "Right on time."

"He brought his own gear," Ernie said to Adam. "You told me he was professional."

"He is, man. He is."

"So why doesn't he know that clubs own turntables?"

"He's particular, that's all."

"Okay, I'm putting this stuff down," Matt said, looking around for somewhere to drop the turntables. Adam grabbed them, one in each hand, and placed them on a table near the door. Ernie crossed his arms and looked at the turntables like they were flattened-out turds. He was an older guy, likely in his fifties. Kind of round in the middle and balding. You had to wonder what he was doing running an all-ages club.

"There are turntables here, Rob," Adam said.

"Okay."

"So give them a try. If they aren't right for you, then I'll help set these up. Cool?" Adam looked at Ernie.

"Just be ready by nine." Ernie walked away, disappearing into the darkness of the club.

The Technic decks were serious old-school. The felt was worn down, and the needle could have been sharper, but they had a nice weight to them, and the arm still bounced when I dropped it on an LP. The sound came out soft and hollow. I started messing with the mixing board, twisting the bass up, leveling out the mid, tightening the treble. I always went for a specific sound, and it took a lot of tinkering before I was able to nail it.

I got an old Underworld song going and tried to beat-mix a new Kid Cudi remix into it. I'd been practicing this at home but knew it needed to be dialed or I wouldn't use it. Somehow I managed to get the two songs perfectly matched, and the mix was seamless.

"Sweet!" Matt yelled.

"Great sound in here!" I yelled back. The DJ booth was raised above the dance floor. It felt strange to be so high up. I pulled another record out and replaced the Underworld. When I looked up again, Adam was in the middle of the dance floor giving me the thumbs-up. I went back to the turntables, trying to mix the next song in.

I'd just got the next song flowing when someone shoved me hard to the side. I stumbled and tripped over one of my record crates, my headphones popping off as I went down.

"What is this shit?" DJ Sly said. He ripped the needle across the LP. The speakers all snapped with the sound.

"Sly, what are you doing?" Adam yelled from the dance floor.

"What's this all about? Who is this clown?" Sly was looking down at me. He was in a white V-neck T-shirt and too-large jeans. He had one of those oversized brimmed hats on, this one with a giant star on the side.

"That's my brother, man," Adam yelled. "He's filling in for you tonight."

"I don't need no replacement."

"Dude," Adam shouted. Then he walked to the stairs that led to the DJ booth and looked up at us. "Dude, how are you going to play records with a broken wrist?"

"I'll manage."

"Listen, he's only taking half pay. You still get a share." Sly looked at me, then back at my brother.

"I get a say in what he plays. It's still my night."

"Sure, man, sure," Adam said.

"And I'm still going to use the mic. He is not to touch the mic."

"I don't even think he'd want to. Would you, Rob?"

"No. I'm cool," I said, standing up and brushing myself off.

"Whatever," Sly said. Then his face changed, and he looked at my brother again. "You and I need to talk," he said, climbing down from the booth.

"What an ass munch," Matt said, once Sly and my brother had disappeared into the chill room at the back of the club.

"I always thought he'd be way cooler," I said.

"That was not cool," Matt said, shaking his head.

I put my headphones on the mixing board and slid the records back into their sleeves. I was shaking, though I wasn't sure if it was from nerves or because of what had just happened.

Either way, it started to feel like it was going to be a long night.

And it hadn't even started yet.

Chapter Three

Half an hour later, there were people entering the club, knocking snow from their hats, then lining up for the coat check.

I tried to keep my mind off the fact that I was not in my room, practicing. That I was actually playing live. For an audience. I lined up my next five songs in a crate, put my headphones on and bent down over the turntables. I decided I would not look up again until all five of those songs had been played. Then I would check the crowd.

I was three songs in when Sly clambered into the booth and grabbed the microphone.

"You all ready for this!" he yelled. The suddenness of it made me jump. "I said, are you all ready for this?" I was playing Skrillex "Right In." I pulled the record back, scratching out a new beat. Sly pumped his fist. Yelled into the mic, "Tonight is your night, my people. Tonight anything can happen. Tonight is the night for you to step outside of yourself. To let your inhibitions fall away. To do what you want to do. There are no rules here. What is it you want to do? What is it you want to say? Tonight is your night." He hit the fog machine, and the dance floor filled with smoke. I switched to DJ Dean's "It's a Dream."

Sly suddenly put the microphone down without switching it off. The feedback squealed through the speakers. I hit the fader for the mic on the mixing board and went back to the records. Sly punched me on the arm.

"Where's your brother?" he said.

"I don't know," I said. I was trying to concentrate on the mix.

"You haven't seen him?"

"Last I saw, he was with you." Sly stood there looking around the club. I went back to my records, and once I got a new mix going, looked back up. I spotted Adam immediately, chatting up the coat-check girl. I pointed him out to Sly. He jumped down from the booth and disappeared into the crowd.

About an eighth of a second later, Matt was beside me.

"That is so douche," he said.

"The propaganda, or dropping the mic?" I said.

"All of the above." Matt flipped a couple of light switches, then stared out at the dance floor. "Who knew this place got so packed so early. Must be something special happening tonight."

"Yeah," I said. "I'm playing." I laid the next record on the turntable and took in the crowd. Though most people were leaning against the walls or talking in little clusters, there were at least thirty people dancing.

"Did you see that MJM just arrived?" Matt said. I almost knocked the record off the turntable.

"Where?"

"Coat check." Sure enough, Mary Jane McNally was taking off her coat and revealing an outfit so lacking in material that I almost forgot where I was. She was talking to Amanda Palmer. The two of them were covering their mouths with their hands and laughing.

"Your song's running out." I flipped the headphone back over my ear and quickly set up the next track. The beat-match was not amazing, but it worked.

"Close," Matt said. I checked out where Mary Jane had been standing, and she was gone. I scanned the area.

"Where'd she go?"

"She's talking to Sly," Matt said.

"She knows him?"

"Dude, I'm just giving you the news here. No background intel available. My advice to you right now? Play something good." I dropped a Deadmau5 LP onto the turntable and tried to ignore the fact that MJ was out there listening.

I had once come within fifteen seconds of asking Mary Jane out. We'd been standing outside the school. It seemed like a coincidence, but I'd been planning this chance encounter for a week. Mary Jane always waited for Amanda outside the school by the parking lot at the end of the day. However, Amanda was always late. Sometimes there was another girl or two with Mary Jane, but I had noted that on Thursdays she was always alone.

I had set up the chance encounter by starting to ask Mary Jane a question during history class just as our teacher, Mr. Hodson, was entering the room. Leaving me to slowly sit back in my seat and say, "I'll talk to you later."

I'd found her out by the parking lot like I imagined I would. I started the conversation with a deep discussion of Mr. Hodson's sweaty armpits. Her laugh made me tingle all over. I moved on to the success of our girls' volleyball team, of which Mary Jane was a member. And then, right when I said, "So, I was wondering…," which was the beginning of the well-rehearsed full sentence, "I was wondering if you'd like to catch a movie some time," Amanda came out of nowhere, grabbed Mary Jane around the

neck and dragged her a way in a cloud
of "Oh my god, you will not believe."

That was my one chance.

Now, out on the dance floor, Sly had
one arm around MJ's waist. She was
smiling up into his face. I could almost
hear her laughing. If she was into guys
like Sly, I figured I didn't have a chance.

I went back to my records.

"He's gone now," Matt said. "Only
to be replaced by your brother." Now
it was Adam who had his arms around
MJ. It seemed innocent enough. After
all, my brother just turned seventeen,
and MJ is only fifteen. They weren't
dancing or anything. Just talking.

He swung away from her, their
hands attached for an extra moment.

"What's that all about?" I said.

"That's about your brother making
all the moves you wish you could."

"He wouldn't," I said.

"No?" Adam went back to where Sly was talking with one of the bouncers. They banged fists, and then Adam looked up at the booth. He gave me the thumbs-up again, as though nothing had happened. Which, I guess, nothing had.

Chapter Four

Two hours later, my set was coming to an end.

You would never think it, but DJing is incredibly tiring. You've pressed all your emotions and energy into matching each song perfectly and creating a flow of sound and beats.

I took my headphones off and pushed my stack of crates together.

I was sweaty and hot. The bass had flattened out some time during my last mix, so I decided to pitch it up a little. Just as I touched the bass fader, there was a loud snap and all the lights went off at once. The mixing board flared with color for a second, then settled into darkness as well.

I've been in some dark places, but I had never before been this encased in blackness. People were yelling and laughing from the dance floor.

The door of the club opened, and a sliver of light illuminated the front passage.

"Everyone out," someone yelled. "Come on, be orderly about it. Fire regulations says everyone gets out."

"Don't you have emergency lights, man?" Someone else yelled.

"Out." I decided to stand still. A moment later, there was a stumbling and banging on the staircase beside me.

"You blew the power, man," Matt said. I felt a hand on my leg. A second later, another hand grabbed at my crotch.

"Dude!"

"Sorry. Jeez, it's dark."

"That is your excuse, and we are going with it. We shall never speak of this moment again." Everyone had their cell phones out, small white lights guiding them through the darkness.

"What happened?"

"I don't know. I was just shutting down. I don't think it had anything to do with me."

"Quite the way to end a set, my man. You will not be followed," Matt said.

"Think the power will come back on?" Matt had his cell phone in front of him. I watched as he bent down beside the mixing board.

"The streetlights are out too. It must be a full power outage." Someone came banging up the stairs to the booth.

"What'd you do, Robbie?" Adam said.

"It wasn't me."

"Sure it wasn't."

"It looks like the whole neighborhood is out," Matt said.

"That was an all right set," Adam said. For most people, all right means passable. But for my brother, it's the height of all compliments.

"Thanks."

"I talked to Ernie, and he said you might get next week as well." He moved back to the stairs. "Come on, I'll help you get this stuff out of here." He pulled a flashlight from his back pocket.

"It's just these crates," I said. "Matt already put the turntables back in the car. Maybe we should wait, though, in case the power comes back on." We stood silently for a moment.

"In my experience, if the power doesn't come right back on, it's going to be out a long time."

"Yeah," I said. "Okay. I was done anyway."

"Okay, slide the crates over," Adam said. I slid the first crate toward him. As Adam grabbed it, the flashlight shifted in his hand. The beam caught something low against the wall behind the booth.

"Hey," I said. "Wait."

"What?" Adam said.

"There's something here."

"Where?"

"Right there," I said. He moved the beam a little more, and what I'd seen before came back into view.

"That looks like a person," said Adam. I froze. Adam pushed the crate aside and climbed down from the booth.

"Hey, hello?" he said. He trained the light on the person. "Hello? Are you all right?" Matt and I followed him down.

"It's Mary Jane," I said. She looked like she'd fallen asleep.

But not quite.

I rushed over to her and grabbed her arm.

It was cold.

"Mary Jane," I said.

"Is she all right?" Adam said.

"She's cold." I shook her a little. "Mary Jane." She didn't move.

"What the hell?" Adam said. He gave a nervous little laugh and bent down beside her. "She party too hard?" He put a finger to her neck. We all waited a second.

"Shit," Adam said.

"What?"

"Call nine-one-one now!" Adam yelled.

"What the hell?" Matt said. "What's happening?"

Adam gathered her in his arms and ran across the dance floor toward the door.

"I don't know," I said as I took off after my brother.

"Call an ambulance!" Adam yelled. People cursed at him until they saw what was going on, and then everyone got out of the way.

The parking lot was full of people shivering in the cold.

By the time I got outside, Adam was halfway across the lot, still carrying Mary Jane in his arms. A police car swung into the parking lot, and the officers got out. I ran up beside my brother.

"What happened here?" one of the officers asked. The other was on the radio, calling an ambulance, I hoped.

"We just found her like this," Adam said. I scanned the lot looking for Amanda or anyone else who would take the responsibility for her away from us. "Do you know if she's taken anything?" the officer asked.

"Taken anything?" I said.

"Drugs." Adam stood there staring at the officer, Mary Jane still limp in his arms.

"We just found her behind the DJ booth, after the blackout," I said.

"So you were not with her?"

"No," I said. "I'm the DJ."

"And you don't know if she's taken anything." I looked at Adam again. He'd turned a shade of white I'd never seen before.

"No," I said. "We don't." An ambulance pulled in behind the cruiser, and two guys got out. They got Mary Jane onto a stretcher and then started asking questions. Luckily, the police answered for us.

The paramedics did a quick examination, then slid her into the back of the ambulance. They tore away, the siren wailing.

It seemed like it had taken forever for all of this to happen. But when I checked my cell phone, only five minutes had passed.

Adam stood there staring at the departing ambulance. I thought I heard him saying something, though with all the noise, I couldn't be certain. I took a step closer to him. He was saying something.

"She's going to be all right," he said over and over again.

And I started to wonder what the hell was going on.

Chapter Five

For some reason, we were sitting outside the hospital at three in the morning. Matt had gone home while Adam and I loaded all my stuff into Adam's car. Then we'd had to answer the same questions over and over again.

I imagine I looked bored, tired and confused by it all. Adam, on the other hand, looked guilty of something. I had no idea what, but he was nervous and sweaty and kept staring out the window at the blank, white expanse of parking lot.

I figured at the time that it was because being grilled by the police makes anyone feel guilty. Like you must have done *something* or you wouldn't be sitting in the back of a police cruiser.

Adam had then driven silently through the dark, empty streets. Resurrection Falls looked strange in the middle of the night without streetlights or the blue glow from the odd television set behind curtained windows.

The hospital was blazing with light. Big, thick plumes of smoke pumped from the smokestacks on the roof. I could smell the diesel generators running from inside the car.

"What are we doing here, Adam?" I asked.

"What's that girl's last name?" Adam said.

"McNally," I said. Adam repeated it.

"She go to your school?"

"Yeah," I said. "She's in a few of my classes." He nodded to this. He'd shut the car off, and it was beginning to get cold. I wanted to tell Adam about how I lusted after Mary Jane. I could have told him how her hair smelled, because I sat behind her in history and leaned forward now and then to breathe it in. How far too many of my dreams placed her in a starring role.

But then I'd have to get into my asking-her-out scheme. And that would just be embarrassing.

"She nice?"

"Yeah," I said. "Totally." He nodded to this.

"She's pretty."

"Yes," I said. "This is true."

"Shit."

"What?" I said. He shook his head.

"Nothing. I'm going in." I was about to ask Adam why he was going in, but he was already out of the car and crossing the parking lot. I got out and followed.

The bright lights of the hospital entranceway were startling at first.

"Why are we here?" I asked again as the automatic doors closed behind us.

"Just to see."

"See what?" He turned to me. His face was still white. His eyes were red-rimmed, as if he hadn't slept in days. He looked as if he was going to say something but only shook his head.

It was impossible to get information out of anyone at the front desk. No, we weren't family. No, we weren't close friends. We were just the guys who'd found Mary Jane and brought her out of the club and were wondering if she was going to be all right.

Eventually, we gave up and went to the waiting room and sat down.

I hate hospital waiting rooms. I never want to touch anything for fear that I'll pick up some superbug and die for no good reason. So I sat totally upright, my hands clasped in my lap.

There were six other people in the room. Every so often one of them would get up and go off somewhere. He or she would eventually come back shaking his or her head and looking mystified. After a while, by listening to them talk to each other, I realized that it was Mary Jane's family, her mother, father, aunt, sister, cousin and grandfather.

At around four thirty, her father stood up and announced that he was going to get some answers.

"We should go," I said to Adam. He didn't respond. He was staring at a place on the far wall. I was about to suggest we leave again when a bellow echoed down the hall.

It was the worst thing I had ever heard.

If you want to know what it's like to have your insides slowly scraped out, listen to a bellow like this. Mary Jane's mother leaped from her seat and darted out of the waiting room. A second later, I could hear her saying, "No, no, no." Adam shuddered beside me, stood up, slammed a fist into the wall and left.

Outside, I started yelling at him.

"What's going on?" He didn't respond. "Adam. What the hell were we doing in there?" I was certain Mary Jane had died. If I'm honest, I would even say I sensed her leaving. Like there was this giant inhale followed by a long, slow exhale, and she was gone. "Adam!" I yelled again. We'd reached the car. Adam got in and slammed his door. I got in the passenger side.

Adam had his head in his hands. He was shaking and sobbing.

"What is going on, Adam? What were we doing in there? Why were you asking me about her?"

He shook his head and turned the ignition. He dropped the car into gear and drove down a walkway past the pay station.

"What the hell are you doing?" By the time we hit the main road, we were moving at almost double the speed limit. "Adam! Slow down. You're going to get us killed." He swerved to make a turn, and the car shifted sideways. We slid across the road and smashed into a snow-bank. Snow flew everywhere, coming back down and rattling against the roof. Adam tromped on the gas again, but the tires just spun on the ice and snow. He started jamming the car into Reverse, then Drive, over and over again until the air was filled with smoke.

He slammed the steering wheel.

"What the hell is going on, Adam?" He turned to face me. His eyes were filled with water, and tears ran down his cheeks.

"I killed her," he screamed. "All right? I killed her."

"Who? Mary Jane?"

"Who else?"

"What are you even talking about?"

He started pounding on the driver's side window until I thought it was going to shatter.

"I screwed up. Man, did I ever screw up."

"What are you talking about, Adam?" He looked ten years older than he had seconds before. Older than I ever could have imagined him.

"She OD'd," he said. "And I was the one who gave her the drugs."

Chapter Six

"Let's get out of here before someone calls the cops," I said.

"What for?"

"Well, we just rammed into a snow-bank and then spun out on ice for, like, five minutes. Someone might call that in." Adam breathed heavily. "I don't need to have any more interaction with the police tonight, all right? Get out and push.

Come on." I shoved him. I'm not sure if, at first, I shoved him because I was angry or simply to get him to snap out of it.

Later I would know exactly why.

"Screw off," Adam said.

"Get out and push," I said again, hitting him.

He turned toward me. Something rose from deep inside me. I punched him in the face.

"What the hell!" he yelled. He undid his seatbelt and came across the seat at me. He managed to get me pinned with one hand and started hammering on me with the other. I covered my head and face with my hands and arms and bent over. "Why'd you hit me?"

"Because you didn't do anything," I shouted.

"I did," he said, still punching me. "I killed her."

I suddenly shot my left arm out. Caught him under the chin. As he fell back. I undid my seatbelt and rolled out of the car. I crab-walked away from the open door. Adam got out and, holding on to the hood, maneuvered himself around the front of the car. He let go for a second and slipped on the ice, hitting the ground with a sharp, fast exhalation of air.

"You didn't kill her," I yelled. "I don't know what happened, but you didn't shoot her or stab her or strangle her. You didn't kill her." Adam pulled himself up and leaned against the hood of his car.

"I gave her the pill," he said.

"What are you?" I said. "A drug dealer? Is that what you do at the club?"

"No. Not really."

"What then?" I said.

"I just give them to people."

"So you're like, what, an illegal-substance Santa Claus? I don't get it." Every time one of us spoke, the air filled with the warm white clouds of our breath. Whenever we stopped talking, the world seemed entirely silent.

"No. It wasn't like that. It was…" The door of the house we were standing in front of opened. A guy came out in a worn-out bathrobe.

"What's going on out here?" he yelled.

"We hit some ice," I said.

"Okay, so what's all the yelling about?"

"We're on our way," I said. I looked at Adam. "Right?"

"Just trying to get the car out of this snowbank!" Adam called. He turned himself so that his hands were on the hood, with one leg stretched out behind him. "Get in and back it out."

I got into the car and turned the ignition. I put it in reverse and gave it some gas. With Adam pushing, the car popped off the icy patch and out of the snowbank back onto dry pavement. I put the car in Park and slid across to the passenger seat. Adam got in and slammed the door closed.

"Why were you handing drugs out?" I asked.

"It was just something I did, man. It was nothing. I mean, everyone there is on E or something. It's no big deal."

Well, I thought, someone died because of it. So maybe it is a big deal.

"Where were you getting the drugs from?"

"Sly," he said. "And it was just E. Nothing else."

"Was he paying you for doing this?"

"Not really. Not officially or anything."

"How did people pay for the drugs?"

"They gave me the money. But I never kept any of it. I put it in this box." It was beginning to sound ridiculous.

"Man," I said. We were at a T intersection at the end of the suburban area. If we went right, we'd head toward the downtown core. To the left was the highway. "So what are we going to do?"

Adam rested his head on the steering wheel. "I don't know. There's going to be an investigation. As soon as the police start asking who people were getting drugs from, my name is going to come up. I guess that's why Sly had it set up this way. He never talked to anyone about drugs. He never handed anything out or was seen with the money."

I looked out the window. Adam had been used. He knew it and I knew it, but neither of us were going to say it. Adam was the front. The one everyone knew.

The one who had sold Mary Jane the drugs that killed her.

"So what are we supposed to do?"

"We can just leave," Adam said. He looked to the left. It was almost six in the morning. My stomach felt filled with acid. Absolutely nothing was making sense.

"Leave? And go where?"

"I don't know. We can figure something out."

"Just leave Mom? Leave town? Leave everything? No way."

"What other options do we have?" Adam asked.

"What's this 'we' stuff?" I said. "I never had anything to do with it." I regretted saying that the second it escaped my mouth. Adam's face dropped. He had never looked so alone.

"Then hop out, man. Just go."

"I didn't mean it like that," I said. I wondered how much time we had before Adam's name started popping up all over the place. The investigation would be in full swing come morning.

"Man, I'm an idiot," Adam said.

"The police will be looking for the dealer and the supplier," I said. "You're the small fry in all of this."

"I'm the front, Rob. That's what you're not getting here. I'm the guy people know. And..." He stopped. "And everyone knows I'm full of shit a lot of the time. If the police question me and I tell them the truth, they'll have, like, fifty people who'll say I'm a big talker. That I lie all the time. And Sly will be the first one to point the cops my way. He's totally clean in all of this."

"Sly never once gave anyone anything?" I asked. Adam shook his head.

"No, man, it was all me. He never even talked about drugs. What am I supposed to do?" I looked at the road that led to the highway. I could hop out, and Adam could drive away. He could be hundreds of miles from Resurrection

Falls by the time the police came knocking at our door.

He could just leave.

Looking back at it now, I wonder what would have happened had I let him go. Not that it was up to me, really. But he was looking for a way out at that moment. He was looking for permission.

And I made him stay.

Chapter Seven

It was Tuesday before the police landed on our doorstep. I'd been home from school for about an hour when it happened. I had an Xbox controller in my hand. *Grand Theft Auto* was paused on our television.

A burly man in a long coat stood on the front porch.

"Robert MacLean?" he said. A wiry mustache tickled his upper lip. He had no sideburns. In fact, he'd trimmed his hair up above his ear, thus producing negative sideburns.

"Um, yeah?"

"Detective Weir. Can I ask you a few questions?"

"About what?"

He pulled a pad and pencil out. "About the death of Mary Jane McNally. You obviously knew her, right? She was in your class? And you were at the club on the night of her death?"

"We were in the same grade. Some of the same classes as well. I was DJing that night. My friend and I found her."

"What was your relationship with the deceased? You did know she was deceased, correct?"

"I heard, yeah," I said. "We were in a couple of the same classes. And then I found her at the club during the blackout."

Detective Weir looked around me. "Would you mind if I came in? Are your parents home?"

"No, my mother's at work. But, sure, okay, come in." Adam was in his bedroom. His car was in the garage. I dropped the controller on the back of the couch and quickly shut the television off, feeling even more like a criminal suddenly. I led the detective to the kitchen and pulled a chair out for him.

"So you saw her on the night of her death?" Weir asked as he sat down. I was suddenly conscious of the fact that our kitchen was a disaster. Plates and dishes all over the place. Towels on the floor. Splotches of sauces and juices that had been dropped and never cleaned.

"I did. She was just lying there."

"Before you found her, I mean."

"Oh, yeah, that too," I said. "I saw her on the dance floor."

The detective looked directly at me. "Did you sell or give Mary Jane any illegal narcotics?"

I shook my head quickly. Not in an immediate denial but in surprise.

"No, no way," I said.

"It has happened before that the DJ, one of the integral links in a club, is also one of the most proficient drug dealers."

"I'm not the regular DJ. I was just filling in."

He sat back in his chair. "How long have you been filling in?"

"That was my first night."

"I see. And who is the regular DJ?"

"DJ Sly," I said. He nodded to this. I was getting the feeling he was asking questions he already knew the answers to.

"What about your brother?" Detective Weir asked.

"What about him?"

He flipped open a little book. "Adam, right?"

"Yeah."

"He was at the club that night as well. What was his relationship with the deceased?"

"You would have to ask him. I doubt he even knew her. We just found her and—"

"Yeah, see," Detective Weir interrupted, "that's the weird thing. Back at the door, you said it was you and your friend who found her. But we have a written report from your brother. He was the one who carried the deceased out of the club."

"Yeah," I said. "Sure, but my friend Matt was there as well. That's what I meant."

"Is your brother here?"

"No," I lied. "I haven't seen him today."

"Does he have a job around here?"

I stared at Detective Weir for a moment. Maybe a moment too long.

"I don't know," I said. I had no idea what the detective knew, but I wasn't about to tell him that my brother worked, in some capacity, at the club.

"What do you mean you don't know?"

"I'm not sure what he's doing these days."

"What kind of work does he do?" Detective Weir asked.

I paused again. I stared at the table and flicked a cluster of crumbs to the ground. "I don't really know."

"You two not get along or something?" Detective Weir asked.

"Yeah, sure we do. It's just—"

"But you don't know where he works?"

"I'm not sure. He's had a few jobs recently, I guess."

"But you don't know where he is or what he's doing?"

"Yeah. I mean, no."

Detective Weir slid his pad back into a pocket and straightened out his jacket.

"It's a bad thing to have happened," he said, shaking his head. "And it didn't need to. Listen, here's the deal. I don't really care who it was that sold the drugs to this girl. We know what happens at these clubs. It's not like you all live on a different planet than us. But I'm tired of trying to bust these small-time guys. What I want to know is who is making this garbage. That and who is selling it in bulk. I want to shut those guys down. If I can do that, then all these small-time guys will just dry up and figure out something else to do with their limited intellect." He sighed heavily. I couldn't tell if it was all an act or not. "A girl died at that club Friday night. Fifteen years old, and she's dead. You understand?"

"Sure," I said. I thought about Mary Jane. About her high-top Converse sneakers. This sweater she would wear that fit her perfectly. The sound of her voice as she answered a question in history class.

I could feel the tears coming.

"And it shouldn't have happened. The whole school's busted up about this. I know. I've talked to a lot of people. The whole community wants this figured out. We all want to get the guy who's been making this crap."

"Okay," I said. A soft, end-of-day light was coming through the kitchen window.

"Here's my card. You hear anything, you give me a call. Your name will remain anonymous. No one but me will know it was you who called. You understand?"

"Sure," I said again. "But I really don't know anything." The back of my throat felt raw and scratchy. The detective got up and walked out of the kitchen.

"Let your brother know I need to talk to him," he said as he opened the door.

"Why?" I said.

He pushed at his mustache with his thumb and index finger. "I'm following up with everyone who was at the club that night. Your brother is a principal player here. Right?"

"How so?"

"Because he found her and brought her to the ambulance," he said. He gave me a firm pat on the shoulder and turned toward his car.

"Yeah. Right," I said. "Okay." I watched the cruiser pull away from the curb. Then I heard Adam's bedroom door open. He was standing in the dim light of the hallway.

"He gone?" he said.

"Yeah."

"What am I going to do, man?" We'd been waiting for the police to show for four days. I'd even grown a little optimistic that no one would ever arrive. That whatever trail there was between Mary Jane and Adam was too thin. But that obviously wasn't the case.

"They don't really have anything on you," I said.

"Not yet," Adam said. "But they soon will."

Chapter Eight

On Thursday, Detective Weir was on my doorstep again. This time with an arrest warrant.

"I need to talk to Adam, Rob," he said by way of greeting.

"I don't know where he is," I said. And I didn't. He'd left Wednesday morning. He hadn't said where he was going or if he would be back.

"This has been issued for a reason," Detective Weir said, handing me the arrest warrant. "I have come across some information linking your brother to the crime. Adam hasn't called me. And now he's disappeared."

"Not disappeared," I said. "I mean, he might have been here this morning."

Detective Weir looked at me sadly.

"If he comes in and talks, everything will be easier. Okay?"

"Okay," I said.

Then it was Friday night and I was in the DJ booth at The Disco. I was an hour into my set, and Sly still hadn't made an appearance. It felt strange to be there. The strangeness permeated the building.

For my part, it was hard to DJ. Every time I got the crowd going, I flashed back to finding Mary Jane against the wall. I almost felt that if I turned around,

I would see her there again, slumped against the wall.

I'd just put on John Selway's remix of "New Heights" when someone grabbed my ankle. I looked down to find my brother reaching up from behind the DJ booth. He put his finger to his lips and pointed toward the side of the booth.

I popped my headphones off and knelt down.

"Come on," Adam said.

"What's going on?" I said.

"Hit the fog machine."

"Okay," I said. I reached up and shot a thick mist onto the dance floor.

"Come on, hurry," Adam said. I jumped off the edge of the booth and landed in the dense smoke.

"What's going on?" I said.

"We have to get out of here." We'd made it three steps onto the dance floor when the house lights went on and the club was filled with noise and motion.

We snaked through the crowd to the chill room. "This way," Adam said, opening a door that I had never noticed before. I followed him through to a short, dark hallway.

"What's going on, Adam?"

"The police are raiding the club. It's turn-out-your-pockets time."

"I thought they had interviewed everyone already."

"They want to catch people with pills on them. Then they can pressure people into finding out where they got them."

"There's already a warrant out for you. Why did you come here?"

"Because some of the people out there are going to roll on you too." He opened a door and pulled me into a small, smelly room. There was garbage all over the place and a bit of snow and ice on the floor.

"What? I had nothing to do with it." Adam shut the door behind us.

"Sly has put out the word that it was the two of us who were dealing in here. But it's not just coming from him any longer. Everyone is repeating the same thing. MacLean brothers, MacLean brothers."

"What the hell? But…"

"There's no *but* here, Rob." Adam opened a hatch in the wall. It was maybe three feet off the floor and big enough for a large garbage pail to be pushed through. A cloud of foul-smelling air rushed in. Adam stuck his head through the hole, then turned back to me.

"Come on, you go first. I'll hold it open for you."

"Go where first?" I said.

"Into the Dumpster."

"What? I'm not going in there." There was a banging behind us. Then someone said, "Is this a door?"

"Those are the cops, Rob. If they bring us in for questioning, we won't be able to prove anything." I looked at my brother. He seemed really afraid. In the end, after all the lies and half-truths, I trusted him. I trusted that he would never lead me into something bad. And, though I'd never say it to him, I loved him. So I pulled myself through the little hatch and into the Dumpster.

It was disgusting inside. The Dumpster had recently been emptied, but there were still things stuck to the sides and back. My foot landed squarely in what once might have been a meatball sub.

I shuffled to a corner once I was inside, trying to keep as gross-free as possible. Adam came through a moment later and very slowly and gently let the door close behind him.

"What's in here?" someone on the other side of the hatch said. "Ugh, garbage room." It was dark and cold in the Dumpster. But I didn't dare make a sound.

We heard the door to the garbage room shut. Adam turned around and raised himself up to look over the lip of the container.

"I parked on Tenth. I don't see any cops out this side." He turned to me and then linked his fingers together low to the ground. "I'll hoist you over. When you land, head to the bushes along the edge of the parking lot. There's a path there to Tenth. Don't look back, okay?"

"Are you sure we shouldn't just talk to them?" I said.

"They are here for us, Rob. If we go back inside, we'll be taken in for questioning. They have at least one person's word that it's the two of us running a drug ring out of the club. By the end of the night, there'll be a dozen more people willing to back that story up if it gets them out of trouble."

"But it isn't true."

He shook his head. "I'll explain every-thing once we're in the car. Come on, hop out. I'll be able to climb out. Just run and don't look back." I decided to trust my brother once again. Anyway, I was freezing and figured it would look pretty suspicious if I suddenly came crawling through the garbage hole.

I put my foot on Adam's clasped hands, and he hoisted me up to the lip of the container. I rolled over the edge and swung down. The moment my feet hit the ground, I started running and didn't look back.

Not even once.

Chapter Nine

Adam's car was locked, so I ran around and hid behind it. My back pressed against the trunk, I sat breathing heavy clouds into a densely falling snow. My legs were twitching, and I wished I'd thought to grab my coat before leaving.

For some reason, as I was lying there, I started remembering this one time we, as a family, went to this cottage.

It was one of those endlessly sunny August weekends. My brother was likely thirteen at the time, and at night he would tell me these tales about all the things he'd done or seen or was going to do. Even then, I could tell half of them were fantasy. But I let him talk. It seemed to make him happy to be able to just say things.

As we were packing to leave, Adam started telling us all about this crazy fish he'd seen when he dove down deep into the lake. We were standing around the car, and Adam was there dripping wet. He started by saying he'd dove down something like twenty feet. That it was darker down there than he'd expected. But he'd been able to hold his breath for at least two minutes. And in that stillness, he'd seen a fish with giant whiskers and an extended tail and giant teeth. It had to be six or seven feet long and had looked right at him, he said. It had opened its mouth, and he'd been afraid it was going to swallow him whole.

No one said anything.

Our parents had been fighting. I'd been able to hear their raised voices inside the cabin. They had come outside separately, not speaking to one another. Not even looking at one another. Which was when Adam came up and started in on this story.

My father finally pointed at my brother, looked at my mother and said, "And you need to put a stop to this shit."

Our dad moved out the next week, and a year later, he left the country to open up a scuba-diving business in Costa Rica.

What I remember most from that day, though, was Adam saying "It's true!" over and over again until he seemed to believe it himself.

I heard heavy footfalls in the snow.

"Rob," Adam called. I struggled to get turned around and stand up. He yelled again, this time sounding panicked.

"Right here," I said.

He put his key in the driver-side lock and opened the car. "Get in. Let's go."

I ran around the side of the car and got in. It was almost as cold inside the car as it was outside. I wrapped my arms around myself. The wipers whisked away the bit of snow on the windshield.

"You cool?" Adam said.

"More like cold," I replied. He looked in the side mirror and put the car in gear. As soon as we had pulled onto the road, he flipped the heat on higher and started messing with the radio. If he were a smoker, he would have lit up at that moment.

"I don't think there'll be any cops back here," he said.

"What's going on, Adam?" I said.

"Apparently, they hauled Sly in again, and this time he decided to roll on me and say I was the one who gave that girl the drugs."

Which is true, I thought. "And they just believe him?"

"Yeah, well, three other people were brought in who will back him up. Amanda something—a girl who was with Mary Jane when I gave her the E. She also said that Mary Jane had been asking about you on the way in. So they figured you were in on it as well, and I guess Sly just went with it."

"How do you know all this?" I asked.

"A friend of mine called to let me know. They pulled her in too. That's why I came and got you."

"What friend?" I asked.

He glanced over at me. "You think I'm lying?"

"No, it's just…what friend, that's all."

"Rachel Jones."

"Rachel?" I said. "Why'd they pull her in?"

"I don't know, Rob. I didn't dig into her life that deeply. That Detective Weir wants this figured out fast, and I guess he thinks I'm his man."

"Oh," I said. "But—"

"No buts. It's true," he said. "Listen, you don't want to come along, then fine. I'll drop you somewhere. But don't blame me when the police pick you up."

I honestly didn't know whether to believe him or not. But I figured that if he was lying, it was only because he didn't want to be alone.

"So where are we going?"

"We have to talk to Sly. We have to make him change his story."

"You think he'll do that?"

"I can pin some of this on him. I mean, his fingerprints have to be all over the place where the drugs and money were kept." Adam slowed for a stop sign but didn't come anywhere near a full stop.

"Where did he keep the drugs?"

"In the garbage room."

I considered this for a second. "Did you get into the club the same way we got out?"

"Yeah. The cops were already all over the place when I got there."

I had no way to tell if this was true. Everything Adam was saying was muddying the waters.

"If you're thinking that I was sneaking into the garbage room to see if there were any drugs left for me to steal, you can forget it," Adam said. "That's not what I was doing. I've never sold drugs, and I'm not going to start now."

It was what I had been thinking. I had had a vision of Adam driving away from Resurrection Falls with enough pills to sell to put him a long way away from all the troubles here.

The problem was, he had sold drugs. He just hadn't made any money from it.

"So you weren't going to leave?"

"No," he said. "I wasn't. I have to come clean. But so does Sly."

Chapter Ten

"We can't go near Sly in my car," Adam said as we neared the downtown core. "He's been in it a few times. Plus, the police will be looking for it." We were passing the high school.

"Pull in here," I said. Adam turned into the school's driveway quickly. "Go around to the back parking lot. They just put another portable back there. The car will be hidden from the road."

"And how are we going to get to Sly's?"

I pulled my cell phone out and dialed Matt.

"Matt," I said when he answered. "Where are you?"

"Home," he said.

"Come to the high school and pick Adam and me up."

"What? Why?"

"Because we need your help."

"What for? Actually, you know, forget it. I'm not going anywhere."

"We're in serious trouble here, Matt." Adam had brought the car to a stop behind the portable. It was snowing hard enough that the tracks would be covered in the next fifteen or twenty minutes.

"What did he do?" Matt asked.

"I'll tell you when you get here. We'll be out by the bike racks."

"No way, man. I'm not—" I hung up before he could go on.

"He coming?" Adam asked.

"Yeah," I said.

"Did he say he was coming?"

"No. But he will."

Adam shut the car off, and we were dropped into a deep, soft silence.

"Why were you doing it?" I finally asked. Adam stared straight ahead. The snow had really begun to come down.

"Honestly, I was just happy to be for real for once," he said.

"What do you mean?"

"I mean I sometimes talk a good game. I really want things to happen, so I say stuff is going to happen or, like, it already has. I figure if it looks like I've done stuff already, people will see me as useful. This thing with Sly, it was…I don't know, it was just that

I wanted to be that guy for once. The guy who got things done. The guy who got people what they wanted."

"You don't have to be like that."

"Yeah, well, what else am I?" He rubbed a hand across his face. "Come on, let's go meet Matt and see if we can't make this right." He opened the door and got out. I followed.

It seemed colder already. The moon and stars had been blotted out by a thick band of clouds.

"Here," Adam said, pulling his coat off and handing it to me.

"No, I'm cool."

"Look, I got you into this. You shouldn't be the one freezing."

I took his coat and put it on. It smelled like Adam. A smell I'd been living with all my life.

Adam jammed his fists in his pockets and stared at a bike that was chained to the racks.

"Who just leaves a bike here?" he finally said.

"I have no idea," I said.

"Like, what happened to whoever owns this thing? Did he just forget he'd ridden to school? Wouldn't he then walk past here every day and see his bike all covered in snow and think, hey, isn't that my bike?"

"You'd think."

Adam stared at the bike.

"Or was he just tired of the bike?" he asked. "Like, he got a ride home in a car one day and then suddenly he was getting a ride in a car every day, so he just left his bike here because he didn't need it any longer."

"Yeah, I still don't know," I said.

"That's a good bike," Adam said. "It's not even like it's a piece of crap. But it's likely been chained here since, what, November?"

"Probably," I said. He kicked the rear tire, and snow tumbled from the seat and handlebars.

"Who is dumb enough to just leave a bike here. Any ideas?"

"At this school? A lot of guys," I said. "It could have been a girl as well."

Adam shook his head. "No, girls aren't that dumb. Ever. Take the dumbest girl in the world, and there'll be a few thousand dumber guys beneath her."

"A few thousand guys beneath her?" I said. "That sounds kind of crowded."

He laughed and hit me on the shoulder. "You're more of a one-on-one guy, are you?"

"Yeah, that's how I roll," I said. He laughed again. A pair of headlights cut through the snow and moved toward the school.

"Those cop headlights?" Adam said.

"No, those are Matty headlights," I said. "See the way the one jiggles? It's loose, and he's never got it fixed."

"Oh yeah," Adam said. "Looks like a chick that's only wearing half a bra."

"Or something like that." We ran out to the road as Matt pulled up. I opened the passenger-side door and got in while Adam slipped in the back.

"Don't tell me we're doing anything illegal," Matt said. "I swear I'll just take you both home. Or, no, I'll just drop you somewhere and make you walk."

"What the hell are you wearing?" Matt had a giant black hat on, with some kind of Russian symbol on the front. Beneath this he was wearing a pink-and-purple scarf, his father's work jacket and a pair of trackpants. "Do you have flip-flops on too?" I asked.

"I grabbed the first stuff I could find. You seemed like you were in a rush.

And you haven't told me whether we're doing anything illegal yet."

"Nothing illegal, Matt," I said. "We just have to find Sly."

"What are we?" he asked. "Private investigators?"

I gave him a long stare. "No, not at all. But for tonight, let's pretend."

Chapter Eleven

"This is, like, the worst part of town," Matt said as we pulled into the parking lot of a bowling alley.

"Likely," Adam said from the backseat.

"And we're here because?" Matt said.

"Because Sly lives in the apartment building across the street."

"So, go in and talk to him," Matt said.

"His car isn't here," Adam said. "He always parks right out front. I don't want to be standing around out there when he arrives. He'd likely just call the cops."

"Man, I do not like this." Three guys came out of the bowling alley. They were dark shapes against the white of the parking lot. "Like, look at these three," Matt said, checking them out in his side mirror. "They look huge." The figures grew larger as they advanced toward the car. When they passed, I realized that they were likely no older than thirteen. Out past their curfew.

"He'll be here eventually," Adam said.

"What is this all about?" Matt said. We hadn't filled him in on pretty much anything. It was often best to keep Matt in the dark. He was far too paranoid to ever be trusted with the entire truth.

"Sly told the police that it was Adam and I who sold the pills to Mary Jane."

"Why would he do that?"

"Because it was really him," Adam said. "Kind of."

"What do you mean kind of?" Matt said.

"There he is," Adam said. A beat-up-looking Nissan Sentra came sliding down the street, stopping on an angle to the entrance of the apartment building. The door opened, and Sly swung out holding his broken wrist.

"He's alone," I said.

"I'll get to him before he goes inside," Adam said. He opened the door as Sly went into the apartment's foyer. Adam was halfway across the parking lot, the hood of his hoodie covering his head, when Sly pulled his phone from a pocket and started talking on it. He turned and stepped back into the street, then slid back into his car. Adam hadn't even made it across the street as Sly pulled away from the curb.

"Pick Adam up," I said to Matt. Adam had already turned around and was running back toward us. Matt got the car started just as Adam swung into the backseat.

"Follow him," Adam said.

"What?" Matt said.

"Follow him. Don't lose him."

"What if he sees me?" Matt said.

"He's not going to expect someone to be following him. Just try to keep your distance. But don't lose him."

"I can't—"

"Go," I said, giving Matt a slap on the arm. "Just follow him."

"Man, he might have a gun or—"

"He doesn't have a gun," Adam said. Matt started the car and pulled out of the parking lot. A minivan had managed to get between us and Sly. "Keep an eye out at the crossroads in case he turns."

"Okay," I said. "Matt, keep watching. I'll watch on this side."

"I'm just going to drive," Matt said in a higher voice than necessary.

"Okay, man. Okay." We drove straight through the downtown core back out toward The Disco. The minivan stayed between us until Sly finally turned right into a neighborhood dubbed Edenvale.

"Why's he going into suburbia?" Adam said.

"Okay," Matt said. "I am better with this. My piano teacher lives here. No one is going to get shot in Mrs. Murdoch's neighborhood."

"So what's he doing out here?" Adam said. We were moving slowly down the snow-filled streets. It didn't seem like a plow had been by in days. Sly was skidding back and forth on the road.

"It looks like he's still drunk," Adam said.

"Where the hell is he going?" I said. He took a sharp right and gunned up a slight hill.

"Go past this road," Adam said. "Don't turn."

Matt slowed down.

"We'll lose him," Matt said.

"It's a cul-de-sac. There are only three houses up there. Just park here."

Matt pulled over in front of a U-Haul van.

"Who lives up there?" I said.

"I don't know," Adam said. "I did the roofing on the places though. They're mansions. It's also really secluded—the perfect place to have a conversation with Sly."

We jogged up the hill. At the top, there were three houses, just like Adam had said there would be. They were set in a semicircle. Sly's car was in front of the center house. There was no way to look casual up there. No one would be in the area unless they had some business there.

"Let's go see who he's visiting," Adam said. "The kitchen and living room are around the back." There was a tall fence and gate, between us and the backyard. Adam tried the gate but it was locked.

"Hoist me over," he said. "I'll go see."

"I need to see too," I said. I looked at Matt with his ridiculous hat and jaunty scarf. "You stay here. Give us a signal if anyone comes."

"What?" Matt said. "By myself?"

"You'll be cool, man. Give us a lift." Matt laced his fingers together and hoisted Adam over the fence. He then spent a good thirty seconds wiping his hands off.

"Now me," I said. He sighed and laced his fingers together again. When I had ahold of the top of the fence, he said, "What kind of signal?"

"Whatever," I said. I didn't really think anyone was suddenly going to come creeping along the edge of the garage.

"Okay," he said. "I'll think of something." I dropped down to the backyard.

"Like a cat." Matt meowed. "That good?"

"Yeah," I said through the fence. "Perfect." He meowed again, and I followed my brother's footsteps in the snow.

Chapter Twelve

The snow was untouched in the backyard. A light glowed from a large
window. Adam was kneeling just
outside of the light, peering through
the window.

"What's going on?" I said.

"Sly's in there," Adam whispered
back.

"Who else?" I said.

"I don't see anyone." I peeked through the window. Sly was leaning against a counter in the kitchen. He had a beer bottle in his good hand. I started to stand a little taller to try and see what he was looking at. But just as I was getting up to full height, Adam yanked me back down.

"Someone's coming into the kitchen," he whispered. I leaned against the wall and stared out at the blank, white backyard.

"Who is it?" I got myself level with the window and looked in. Standing on the other side of the kitchen from Sly was Amanda Palmer.

"Do you know her?" Adam said.

"Yeah, that's Amanda Palmer. She's one of Mary Jane's friends."

"I thought I recognized her," Adam said. "She was at the club that night, wasn't she?"

"Yeah, they did everything together."

"What's Sly doing with her? I mean, she's like your age."

"And Sly's, what, eighteen?"

Adam looked at me as if I were dim. "Twenty-one."

"No way."

"Yeah."

I looked through the window at Amanda. She was wearing a tank top and pajama bottoms. Her hair was all over the place, and she looked as if she'd been crying.

"Do you think something was going on between him and Amanda?" I whispered.

Adam shrugged. "I have no idea."

Amanda was shaking her head at whatever Sly was saying. Sly held his hands out to her, and she backed up, wrapped her arms around herself and then pointed at the front door. Sly dropped the beer bottle onto the counter and took a step toward her. She backed up again, and I heard her yell, "Just go."

"What's he doing?" I said.

"I don't think she wants him there," Adam said.

We watched as Sly reached out for her. She turned away from him, and he grabbed her roughly and spun her around.

"The asshole," Adam said. And then he was up and running toward the front of the house. Amanda shoved Sly away, and he came right back at her, grabbing her and shaking her.

I followed Adam around the side of the house and scurried over the fence.

"What's going on?" Matt said.

"Sly's getting weird with Amanda Palmer," I said as I dropped to the ground.

"Amanda? What's she doing with him?" I darted past Matt, trying to keep up with my brother.

I made it to the porch to discover the front door open. I hesitated for a moment and then stepped in.

The house was dark except for the kitchen and living room. It seemed that Sly spotted Adam just as I came out of the foyer.

"What are you doing here?" Sly said.

"You have to tell the truth," Adam said.

"Amanda, you'd better call the police," Sly said. He let Amanda go and pointed at the cell phone on the counter. "There's a criminal in your house."

"Everyone just get out," Amanda said.

I came up behind my brother.

"Two criminals," Sly said. He smirked at me. "Drug dealers, or so I've heard."

Adam stepped toward Sly. Amanda grabbed the phone. Her eyes were all over the place, dancing from one of us to the next. She suddenly ducked into the hallway saying, "Yes, police please."

"You know my brother had nothing to do with it," Adam said.

"That's not what I hear," Sly replied. He zipped his coat up and moved around the island that separated the kitchen from the living room. "Listen, why don't you just get out of here. The police are going to be here any minute, and they have an arrest warrant on your head."

"Because I'm not going to run," Adam said. "I'll cop to my part in all this, but you have to as well."

"I don't have to do shit, man." He laughed and casually put his hands in his pockets. "You are such a chump. What did you think was going to happen?"

"I didn't think anyone was going to die."

"Yeah," Sly said. "That's not really anyone's plan, is it. But someone did." Sly moved past Adam, almost as though he was daring him to make a move."

"You're going to admit you were the supplier," Adam said.

"Who, me? I have no idea what you're talking about."

"Your fingerprints have to be all over that garbage room."

"You mean the one at the club? Well, sure, I work there, right?" Sly shook his head.

I saw my brother's fists clench. Sly did too.

"My brother had nothing to do with it," Adam said.

I could hear sirens in the distance. Everyone turned and looked at the door as though the police would already be standing there waiting.

"I already told you, I don't know what you're talking about." Sly laughed again.

And a moment later, Adam was on him. He caught him in the side of the head with a big full swing. He followed this with a jab to the gut and, as Sly started to go down, he caught him with an uppercut. I had never seen my brother move so quickly before.

Sly fell to his knees. Adam took a step forward and kicked him in the chest, then jumped on top of him once he was on the floor.

"My brother had nothing to do with it."

"What is wrong with your head, man?" Sly said. He turned sideways and spit out some blood.

"Adam," I said. "Let him up before the cops get here."

Amanda came back into the room.

"Say it," Adam said. "Say it so everyone can hear it. My brother had nothing to do with it."

"Fine. As far as I know, he had nothing to do with it," Sly said.

Adam turned to Amanda. "Did you hear that?"

"Yeah," she said.

"You'll tell the police?"

"Sure," she said. I noticed that she never once looked at me. "I knew that."

"You tell them," Adam said. Blue and red lights flashed around the room. There was a slamming of car doors. Adam stood. As the officers stepped into the room, he raised his hands.

"Everyone stay still," one of the officers said.

"This guy just assaulted me," Sly said. He'd pulled himself up onto a chair and sat there shaking.

"I am Adam MacLean and I want to confess to my crimes," Adam said. One of the officers crossed the room and grabbed Adam's hands. He pulled them down and cuffed him, then patted him down for weapons.

"I want to press charges," Sly said, spitting blood onto the carpet. The officer walked Adam out of the living room.

"Everyone stay put," the other officer said. "We might be here awhile."

Chapter Thirteen

Adam came home for two days before the police arrived to take him for his first of many court appearances. There were a lot of charges against him. Dealing drugs was at the top of the list. Assault came a close second. Adam told the police the same story, the one where Sly had him handing out the drugs and nothing more, over and over again, but no one wanted to listen. The problem was he'd lied to them before. He'd run away. And it was only at the last minute that he came clean about giving Mary Jane the drugs that had killed her.

I felt like that was the most courageous thing he had ever done. No matter what happened, it seemed to me that Adam had redeemed himself with that one admission. He could have gone on lying. In fact, he might have got away with it. But he finally stopped telling stories and, instead, admitted to his part.

Amanda told the police that, to her knowledge, I had had nothing to do with drugs at the club. But she had also been there when Adam had given Mary Jane the drugs that killed her. I later heard that she'd had something going with Sly. Though, whether she knew he was the actual dealer or not, I'll never know. Sly had kept himself well removed from the whole enterprise.

Once it was all said and done, there was no way to prove he'd ever even seen a bag of drugs before.

Two months after the incident, Adam was in jail. There was no doubt this was going to happen. He'd been caught in the middle, and though he hadn't intentionally done anything to hurt anyone, someone had died. Detective Weir had worked hard to make certain Adam was not out on the streets. I think he figured Adam would, eventually, roll on whoever the distributer was. And he had. Over and over again. Sly was the center. Sly was the real dealer. Sly had put him up to it. But that wasn't the answer the detective wanted.

It sounded too much like another lie.

There's a lot that goes into being a visitor at a prison, even a juvenile one. Luckily, since visiting hours were almost over, I was able to pass through with a little of my dignity intact.

Adam was sitting at a table in the middle of the visitors' room.

"No Plexiglass shield between us?" I said as I sat down. He was in an orange jumpsuit. The room was filled with low, murmured conversations and occasional sobs. It was, by far, the very worst place I had ever been in my life.

"Yeah, that's only for the hard-core guys," Adam said.

"Hey, don't kid yourself. You're hard-core."

"Not so much in here, Rob." He looked at me, then turned his head away. "This place is awful."

"Yeah," I said. Our mother had been to visit once. I'd been at school that day, so this was the first time I'd spoken with Adam since he'd been put in here. "But you won't be here for long."

"Who knows?"

"Is it really bad?" He nodded to this, his head tilted down. I could tell he was crying, and I had no idea what to do. I wanted to reach over and hold him. To give him a hug, like he used to do for me when we were young and I'd fallen and hurt myself. He used to be able to make anything better. And yet now, I could do nothing for him.

"So," I said.

"Sorry, man. It's just…" He looked up, then away. "It's not where I expected to be, you know?"

"Yeah," I said. "I know."

"It's just so stupid. Everything. Why?" He stopped, shook his head again. "The counselor says asking why isn't useful. Not now. Anyway, I know why."

"Why what?"

"Why I'm here."

"And why is that?"

"Because I'm a bad person."

"No, you're not," I said. "Man, not even close. You made a bad choice. That's all. This will blow over, man. This is nothing. You never received any money for any of the drugs."

"Sly paid me."

"Not for that," I said.

"Yeah, well, the problem is that I have a certain reputation. Anytime anyone asks about me, the first thing they hear is that I'm full of shit. That doesn't help when I claim I'm innocent. And it wouldn't even matter if they got something on Sly. It wouldn't change any of the facts."

"How's your lawyer?"

"I don't know. I haven't really spoken to her."

"They can't keep you here for long."

He looked at the table again. "Mandatory sentence," he said. And those were the two hardest words he'd likely ever had to say. And the two hardest I had ever heard.

"Something will happen," I said.

"Yeah." He looked at me again. "Listen, don't take this the wrong way, but it'd probably be best if you didn't come visit."

"What?"

"I don't want you around all this shit."

"Adam. I will be here every week."

"Man, don't do that. We can talk on the phone, all right?"

"No, I mean, yeah, but also…"

"It's just going to be for the best." He suddenly stood up. "I'm sorry, man. I should have tried harder."

"Tried harder at what?" I said.

"Just, you know, tried harder. Tried to be someone rather than create the illusion of someone."

"You're someone," I said. "You're my brother."

"Yeah." He smiled and gave me a nod.

"You maybe need to choose your family a little better next time."

But that isn't an option, I thought. We don't choose our family.

"Given the choice," I said, "I'd still choose you."

"Proving yet again that your grades do not necessarily reflect your intelligence." He gave me a slight smile. "Listen, I just don't want you to see this shit. I don't want you to be here around these people. It won't do you any good. Forget about me for now. I'll see you when I get out, and maybe we can start again." He turned to leave.

And though there were signs everywhere that read No Touching, I couldn't stop myself. I couldn't just let him go off like that. Even in those final moments, I had to try and make things better. I darted around the table and grabbed him and held on to him as hard as I could.

"I'm sorry, man. I should have tried harder too. I'm sorry."

"No touching!" someone yelled. But I just held on. "Hey, no touching." Then there were hands on me, pulling me away.

And, a moment later, he was gone.

Jeff Ross is the author of three books in the Orca Sports series—*Dawn Patrol, The Drop* and *Powerslide*. He was a DJ for a number of years but now lives happily, although with reduced hearing, in Ottawa, Ontario, where he teaches Scriptwriting and English at Algonquin College.

orca soundings

The following is an excerpt from
another exciting Orca Soundings novel,
Dead Run by Sean Rodman.

9781459802445 $9.95 PB
9781459802452 $16.95 LIB

BICYCLE RACING IS SAM'S SPORT, AND HE
wants to win—no matter what it takes. So
Sam signs on with Viktor, an aging Olympic
medalist, as his coach. But there's a catch.
Sam has to work as a bicycle courier at Viktor's
company, making deliveries in downtown traffic
at breakneck speeds. Then he is assigned the
"dead run," delivering untraceable packages
for an unknown client. Soon Sam is racing away
from the law—and risks losing everything.

Chapter One

I have no fear.

I'm tensed and ready, like a coiled spring. I know that the stakes in this race are high. But I am not afraid. I'm totally focused. Nothing exists except the starting signal. And the bike beneath me.

The light goes green. I hammer down, making powerful sweeps with my pedals, surging forward. The BMW to my left starts to accelerate, but I beat him into the intersection. Then I'm across the street. Dodging around a big green Dumpster. Weaving back away from a city bus.

In my mind, I'm ahead of the pack at the Olympics. I'm fighting it out with the best cyclists in the world. But it's all in my head. So far. The truth is that I'm only seventeen, with just a couple of races under my belt.

It's a start. I've got big plans.

A delivery truck blocks my lane, so I bunny-hop onto the sidewalk. I pull up in front of Quan's Groceries, leaning my steel-gray racing bike up against a metal grate. I slap my lock around the bike and the grate, then walk in.

"Hey, Sam," grunts the big guy behind the counter.

"Hey, Mr. Lee," I reply. "Just need some breakfast."

"Are you in that bike race downtown today?" Mr. Lee asks. Me and my dad are regulars here.

"Yeah, the Albion Square Crit. I'm on my way." I carefully pick out two of the least spotted bananas from the display.

"You going to win?"

I come back to the counter. "You can bet money on it," I say. Mr. Lee chuckles.

"Then the bananas are on the house today. Consider it my big sponsorship for you."

I laugh and thank him. Outside, I slide the bananas into the wide pocket at the rear of my jersey. I check my watch—damn, I'm late again. Gotta move it. I'm on the bike and back on the road. Fighting through traffic. Racing.

Big sponsorship. That would be nice. I'm still in the Junior category. Which means no real money, not like the pros. Mind you, today is a little different. The Albion Crit—short for "criterium"—

is a city race, ten laps around a couple of blocks downtown. Like most races, there's an individual winner as well as a winning team. But in this crit, there are also special prizes. The judges will ring a bell in the middle of the race. That means whoever wins the next lap gets $100. A little extra money would be kind of a big deal right now. Things are pretty tight at home. Dad works the night shift at a warehouse, which barely pays our rent. Mom—she left a couple of years ago.

My focus snaps back to the street when I see the red brake lights of a taxi flare in front of me. I lean hard, dodging a woman stepping out of the yellow cab. Don't want to get doored.

By the time I get to Albion Square, there's a big crowd waiting at the start line. It's drizzling a little now, a fine mist that slicks the road. I walk my bike in between the brightly colored rain jackets and umbrellas, looking for my team.

There they are—two guys working on their bikes, both my age. The tallest one looks over.

"Sam!" Hayden says loudly. "What took you so long?"

"Traffic," I say.

"Whatever," Hayden says. He straightens up and looks at me. "It's always something." His black hair is plastered to his head with the rain. He's clearly not in a good mood. "And you didn't show up for practice last night. What was your excuse for that?"

"No excuse. I didn't need the practice. My time is good," I say. I look him right in the eyes, daring him to take me on. Christ, Hayden's annoying. His dad owns a bike shop, which means we get free gear. Gear that I can't afford. But Hayden thinks that also means he's the coach. We lock tough-guy stares for a minute. Then he breaks it off.

"All right, this is the plan. It's Andrew's turn to take the lead. You and I will cover him, let him draft behind us. We all hold back for the first eight laps. Then Andrew will break away and go for it."

"That doesn't make any sense," I say. "Andrew isn't a sprinter. We'll lose."

"Actually, he's right," Andrew says to Hayden, shrugging. "Sam is a way better sprinter than me…" He's a small kid, always a little nervous around me.

"You don't get it, Sam," Hayden says. "If we don't give Andrew the chance, he's never going to get better, right? It's not like this crit is a big deal. It's just practice."

"Now we're practicing to be losers?"

"Enough. You want to race today or not?"

I do. And as much as I hate Hayden's attitude, if I want to keep racing on the team, I don't really have a choice. I suck it up.

"Fine," I say. "Andrew takes the breakaway."

Twenty minutes later, we're at the starting line. The street is clogged with brightly colored racers. I recognize a few of the teams. The Red Rock Cycles guys are hard to miss in their red-and-white uniforms. They have the best bikes and pretty much always place in the top rankings. There's part of me that wants to beat them. And part of me that wishes I were on their team.

Time to pull it together. I take some deep breaths, trying to slow down my heart, riding the adrenaline building in my veins.

The noise of the crowd suddenly drops. There's a long blast from an air horn. Immediately, the pack of cyclists crashes forward across the line. It's all pistoning legs, elbows out, just trying to stay upright. One guy spills into the crowd as we go around the first corner.

The pack starts to stretch out, the slowest riders dropping behind while the best ones pull ahead. By the time we're in the straightaway, my team is right in the middle of the pack.

Six laps later, we're still in the middle. I'm pulling for Andrew, who is drafting behind me. Hayden and I have been taking turns letting him ride close to our bikes, practically touching wheels. By cycling like this, we make it easier for him to pedal and conserve his energy. That way, he should be rested and ready for his big break. If he's still up for it. I shoulder-check, then drop back to talk to him.

"Next lap, you ready?" I say. Andrew can't speak, he's panting so hard. He just nods and grunts. This plan is not going to work. I look ahead as the pack dives into the straightaway on our eighth lap. On the sidelines I see one of the race organizers lift a big silver bell and ring it.

There it is. Winner of the next lap gets one hundred bucks.

Screw it.

I rise up off my seat and push down, hard. In seconds, I'm away from Hayden and Andrew. My chest starts to heave. I focus on the leader, on the back of his Red Rock Cycles jersey. A moment later, I'm beside him. Then I'm on my own and headed to win that hundred bucks. And maybe the race. If I can stay ahead of the pack.